USBORNE HOTSHOTS
RIDING

USBORNE HOTSHOTS
RIDING

Edited by Gina Walker
Designed by Karen Tomlins

*Illustrated by Eric Rowe, Fred'k. St. Ward,
Gordon King, Norman Young, Joan Thompson
and Rhoda Burns*

*Photographs by Kit Houghton
and Only Horses Picture Agency*

Consultants: Patricia Smyly and Susanne Frank

Series editor: Judy Tatchell
Series designer: Ruth Russell

*With thanks to Christopher Rawson,
Joanna Spector and Elizabeth Polling*

CONTENTS

About your pony

Riding is a lot of fun. To get the most out of it, you need to know how to ride safely and well, from sitting properly in the saddle, to galloping and jumping.

Measuring a pony

The height of a pony is measured in centimetres or hands from the ground to the top of the pony's withers. One hand equals about 10cm (4in). Take off 1cm (½in) to allow for the pony's shoes.

Poll

Cheekbone

Withers. The withers should not be too flat, or your saddle will slip.

Forelock

Muzzle

Neck. The neck should be longer on top than underneath, for good balance.

Shoulder. Long, sloping shoulders mean the pony will be comfortable to ride.

Chest. A deep, broad chest gives room for a strong heart and lungs.

Cannon. A short cannon bone means the leg is strong.

Elbow

Knee

Forelegs

Catching a pony

1. Enter the field and shut the gate. Take a head collar and some treats. Call the pony.

2. Walk to the pony, talking softly. Offer a treat and slip the lead rope over its head.

Parts of a pony

The picture below shows the names of some of the main parts of a horse or pony.

Back. A short back is stronger than a long back.

Loins. The weakest part of the back is just behind where the saddle goes.

Hindquarters

Dock

Flank

Point of hock

Thigh

Hindlegs

Hooves should be hard and strong.

Heel

Fetlock

Pastern. The pasterns should be long and sloping to act like shock absorbers.

Pony colours

Here are some common pony colours.

Black

Grey

Skewbald

Chestnut

Dun

Bay

Brown

3. Put on the head collar. Give the pony a pat and another treat, as a reward.

4. Take the rope. Say "Walk on" and lead the pony from beside its shoulder.

Saddles and bridles

Saddles, bridles and other pieces of riding equipment are called tack. Tack costs a lot, but if you take care of it, your tack will last for many years.

Pommel

A saddle with a deep seat is more comfortable than a flat one.

Cantle

The saddle

Stirrup bars. These attach the stirrup leathers to the saddle. The safety catch must be kept down.

Stirrup leathers. Check these regularly for signs of wear.

Stirrup. Run the stirrups up the leathers when you are not using the saddle.

Saddle flap

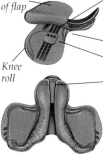

Underside of flap

Knee roll

Girth straps. The girth buckles onto these.

Thigh roll

Buckle guards

Hollow channel, or gullet, to keep the rider's weight off the pony's spine.

The saddle has a frame, or tree.

Cleaning the saddle

Clean your saddle after every ride. Take off the girth and stirrups. Sponge off the dirt with a damp sponge. Dry the leather, then rub in saddle soap. Polish the stirrups and clean the girth. Lastly, put everything back in place. Every year, have the saddle checked by a saddler.

Saddling up tips

Put the saddle over the withers and slide it back into place. Fasten the girth.

Some ponies puff out their chests, so check the girth again before you get on.

A saddle should not touch the pony's spine, even when you are sitting on it.

The bridle

The reins on your bridle should be about 1½cm (¾in) wide. Make sure the reins are not too long, or you may catch your feet in them.

Headpiece. The cheekpieces buckle onto this.

Throatlash

Browband. This stops the headpiece from slipping back.

Noseband

Cleaning the bridle

Wash the bit after every ride, so food and saliva do not dry on it. Undo all the buckles and wipe each piece separately. Dry them with a clean cloth, then rub in saddle soap with an almost dry sponge. Put the bridle back together, ready to use.

Reins

The cheekpieces must be level on each side and hold the bit in the corners of the mouth.

Bit. A correctly fitted bit just creases the corners of the pony's mouth.

Tips on bridling

Open the pony's mouth gently with your thumb, and push in the bit.

Check that the bit is level before fastening the noseband and throatlash.

You should be able to fit your hand under the throatlash, like this.

Getting on and off

Getting on a pony is called mounting. Before you mount your pony, make sure that the girth is tight enough or your saddle may slip around. Always put your hard hat on before you mount your pony.

You need to be able to tighten the girth with one hand.

When mounted, check the girth again before you begin to ride. Move your leg forwards and lift the saddle flap. Tighten the straps by pulling them up one at a time. Push the spike of the buckle into a higher hole.

Mounting

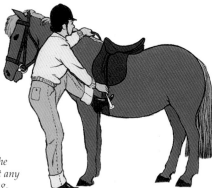

1. Stand by your pony's left shoulder, facing the tail. Hold the reins in your left hand, with a handful of mane. Hold the stirrup with your right hand and put the ball of your left foot into the stirrup.

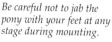

Be careful not to jab the pony with your feet at any stage during mounting.

2. Spring up as lightly as possible. Hold onto the front of the saddle with your right hand.

3. Swing your right leg over your pony's back. Be careful not to touch the pony with your leg.

4. Sit down gently into the saddle. Put your right foot into the stirrup and take up the reins.

To adjust the stirrups, pull the loose end of the stirrup leather, holding one finger on the spike of the buckle. Now you can move the leather up or down, without losing the end.

Hold the reins lightly, with your thumbs on top.

The reins should pass between your third and little fingers and be held between your thumbs and first fingers.

Dismounting

Getting off a pony is called dismounting. It is dangerous to dismount by swinging your leg over the pony's neck. Here is the correct way to do it.

Let both legs hang free before dismounting.

Lean forwards slightly before you dismount.

1. Take both feet out of the stirrups. Put the reins in your left hand. Put your weight on your right hand on the front of the saddle.

2. Lean forwards on your right hand and swing your right leg clear over the pony's rump.

3. Being careful not to kick the pony's back, land on both feet with knees bent. Run up the stirrups.

4. Take the reins over the head. Hold them close to the bit, with the buckle end in the other hand.

Walking and trotting

Ponies have four paces – walking, trotting, cantering and galloping. These are described on the next four pages.

Walking

Walking is the easiest pace because it is calm and steady. You have time to think about the right way to ride. Relax just enough to feel the rhythm of your pony's stride.

Try not to lean or look down.

Hold the reins lightly. They are there to control and guide the pony, not to hold you steady.

Follow the movement of your pony's head with your hands.

Sit well down in the saddle and relax your hips.

How a pony walks

A pony's walk has four hoof beats. Each hoof strikes the ground in turn, as shown below.

Left foreleg.   *Right hindleg.*   *Right foreleg.*   *Left hindleg.*

10

Trotting

Trotting is more bouncy than walking. It can feel uncomfortable until you learn to rise in time with the pony's movements. Let the bounce of the stride push you up and forwards a little from your lower leg. Then sit back gently in the saddle in a regular rhythm.

It may help to say, "Up, down" in time with your pony's stride.

Keep your head up and looking to the front.

Do not try trotting until you feel balanced and confident when walking.

Try to keep your hands and lower legs still.

Keep your back straight, but not stiff.

How a pony trots

Trotting has two hoof beats. Opposite pairs of hooves, front and back, strike the ground together. These are called diagonals.

Left foreleg and right hindleg.

Other pair moves forward.

Right foreleg and left hindleg.

Other pair moves forward.

11

Cantering and galloping

Cantering is exciting and is the pace which most riders like best. It is tiring, so try cantering for just short periods to start with. You will be stiff at first, and find it hard not to bounce up and down. To begin with, hold the saddle with one hand.

Hold the reins so that you allow the pony's head to swing up and down with the stride.

Allow your hips to go with the movement of the pony, so your seat stays in the saddle.

Sit up straight.

If you are riding on a bend, the inside leg should lead (see below), so your pony is balanced.

How a pony canters

A canter has three hoof beats. A pony can canter with either foreleg leading. This is the leg that is seen out in front of the pony as it canters. This leg lands on the third beat.

Left hindleg.   *Right hindleg and left foreleg.*   *Right foreleg comes forwards (leading leg).*   *Right foreleg (leading leg).*

Galloping

Galloping is the fastest, most exciting pace. You should gallop only if your pony is fit, and you can control it when cantering. A pony increases its speed from canter to gallop by taking longer strides. It pushes harder with its hindlegs, and stretches out its body. Each foot is on the ground for a shorter time, and there is a moment when all four feet are off the ground.

Take your body forwards and out of the saddle. Have your stirrups shorter and your weight on your knees and feet.

If you are on a bend, make sure the inside leg leads, as when cantering.

Never gallop where there are people walking.

How a pony gallops

A gallop has four separate hoof beats. A pony can gallop with either foreleg leading, as in a canter. This leg lands on the fourth beat.

Right hindleg.   *Left hindleg.*   *Right foreleg.*   *Left foreleg (leading leg).*

Controlling your pony

A well-trained pony has been taught to understand a set of signals that the rider uses to tell it to change pace or direction. These signals are called aids. You use your voice, hands, body and legs to give the aids.

Keep your head up and look straight ahead.

Your back should be straight but not stiff.

Sit with your knees and thighs close against the saddle.

Voice

Talk quietly but firmly. Your pony should understand simple commands like "walk", "trot" and "whoa", but not long sentences.

Hands

Your hands help to control and guide the pony. Use your fingers to send messages along the reins.

Body

You can give your pony messages by shifting the pressure of your body slightly on the saddle.

Legs

Use the lower part of your legs just behind the girth to tell your pony to go faster.

Exercises

It may seem difficult and tiring at first to ride the right way. This is because you are using muscles which do not often have to work. Try these exercises to help make you supple. Do them with someone to hold your pony. Knot your reins so you don't catch your feet in them.

Rising in the saddle

Push down and raise your seat about 5cm (2in) from the saddle. Then lower it gently.

Keep your hands just above the withers.

Holding the reins

Hold the reins lightly, with your hands about 10cm (4in) apart, so you can just feel your pony's mouth. Never pull hard at the reins or use them to help keep your balance. This will make the pony's mouth hard and it will soon begin to ignore your hand aids through the reins.

Sit in the middle of the lowest part of the saddle.

Squeeze your pony's sides just behind the girth – never kick. Pressure farther back behind the girth helps to control the pony's hindquarters, telling it when to move sideways or turn.

Your knees and ankles act like springs. Don't let them become tense.

Rest the ball of your foot on the stirrup. Keep your heels down.

Toe touching

Bend down and touch your toes on each side. Keep your legs still.

Around the world

Swing your right leg over the pony's neck. Swing your left leg over its back.

Continue in the same direction, one leg at a time, until you are facing the front again.

Changing pace

Changes from one pace to another should be smooth. Signal your intentions clearly and gently to the pony. Some ponies need stronger aids than others, but try to keep your signals subtle.

Increasing pace

Halt to walk
Squeeze with your lower legs and say, "Walk on". Release pressure on the reins slightly. If the pony tries to move before you give the signal, stop it by increasing the pressure on the reins.

Hold your head up.

Keep a light contact with the pony's mouth.

Sit up straight without becoming stiff.

Walk to trot
Shorten the reins, then squeeze with your legs to signal that you want to increase the pace. For a smooth change from a walk to a trot, sit the first few strides. Start to rise once your pony is trotting in a steady rhythm.

Keep your heels low, and rise from your knees.

Repeat the leg pressure to keep a steady pace.

Trot to canter
Sit deep in the saddle and push with your seat. To canter with the right leg leading, pull gently on the right rein, and give firm pressure with your left leg behind the girth. To canter with the left leg leading, do the opposite.

Sit deep in the saddle.

Use your inside leg on the girth to keep the pony going.

Decreasing pace

Before you decrease the pace, think about the rhythm of the pace you want to change to and start to slow your body into that rhythm. Your pony will feel the signals from your body.

Canter to trot

Straighten your back and lengthen your legs. At the same time, gently increase your feel on the reins, and slowly say, "Trot". Keep your legs close to the pony's sides, and bring it to a smooth trot.

When you feel the pony respond, relax your fingers.

Sit still, so you do not unbalance your pony.

Trot to walk

Stop rising to the trot and straighten your back. Gently increase your feel on the reins, and slowly say, "Walk". Bring your legs close against the pony's sides, to keep it moving in a lively rhythm as it slows to a walk.

Do not let your feet slip forwards.

Push down into your heels.

Walk to halt

Straighten your back, and increase your feel on the reins, saying, "Whoa". Press with your legs to bring the pony's hind legs under its body. Aim to halt with the pony's front and back legs square with each other.

Remember you are asking the pony to stop, not pulling it to a standstill.

17

Changing direction

These pictures explain how to turn your pony smoothly to the right. To turn to the left, follow the instructions, but on the opposite side. Sit up straight and keep your seat square in the saddle, or you will unbalance the pony.

Turning to the right

The pony should bend its neck and spine as well as its head.

Look, but don't lean, in the direction you want to go.

Increase the pressure on the right rein. Release the left rein slightly to allow the head to turn.

Use your left leg lightly a little farther back than usual. This stops the hindquarters swinging out.

The right leg stays close to the girth. The pony should seem to bend around this leg as it turns.

Hind feet should follow in the tracks of front feet.

Changing the rein

When you change the rein, you turn and ride in a different direction. You need to be able to change the rein smoothly, without changing the pony's rhythm. The best place to exercise is in an enclosed arena, or school. The standard size is 20m x 20m (66ft x 66ft). Certain points around the school are marked with letters. These are always the same in any school, so try to learn them by heart.

The picture shows a school, with two different ways to change the rein. You can go diagonally across the school as shown in blue, or straight across as shown in red.

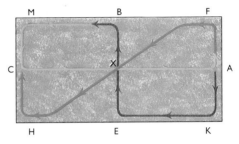

Below are some more exercises which will help to improve your turning technique. Imagine a path drawn on the ground with the turns you want to make. Look in the direction you want to go.

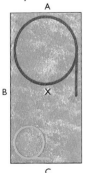

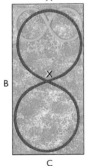

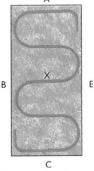

Start with large circles. They are easier to do than small, tight ones.

A figure-of-eight is like two circles with a change of rein in the middle.

A serpentine is very good practice for changing the rein. Keep the loops even.

Improve your riding

You and your pony need to work together as a team if you want to be able to ride really well. On the next four pages are some of the things you need to practise to achieve this.

Impulsion

Your pony should feel as if it has energy stored up in its hindquarters, ready for you to drive the pony on at your command. This is called impulsion.

You will be able to create impulsion in your pony only if you have a strong, balanced seat. This leaves your lower legs free to make your pony move forwards energetically. A good way to help you do this is by trotting on the lunge without holding the reins and without your feet in the stirrups. This will improve balance and leg position.

Why you need impulsion

An untrained pony may feel as if it is going to stop unless you keep nagging at it with your heels.

It carries most of its weight over its forelegs. It does not use its hocks and hindleg muscles to push it forwards.

A well-trained pony has learned to carry more weight on its hindlegs. It moves more freely and is easier to control.

Carriage

Carriage describes how your pony moves and carries its weight and yours. As training progresses and the pony's hindquarters do more work, the pony will begin to carry itself well and look more relaxed and confident.

Your pony will not have good carriage unless it can accept the bit. This means letting the bit rest against the sensitive sides of its mouth without resisting.

To help the pony accept the bit, gently squeeze your fingers on the reins. Then relax them as the pony accepts the pressure.

Common faults

Above the bit
The pony carries its head high to avoid the bit. Its neck is stiff so it is hard to control.

Behind the bit
The pony shortens its neck and lets go of the bit, avoiding your signals.

Overbent
The pony tucks its head in to its chest and pulls against the rider's hands.

Poking the nose
A stiff jaw and straight neck may be due to a pony not using its hindlegs correctly.

Raising its head

Do not pull the pony's head up. Use your legs to get its hindlegs under it. This will make its front lighter and raise its head.

21

Suppleness

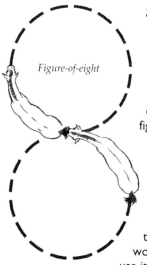

Figure-of-eight

A supple pony will be able to change pace and direction without getting unbalanced. The pony may be stiffer on one side and you will have to do more work on that side. A good exercise for suppleness is to trot a figure-of-eight. Your pony bends its spine first one way and then the other.

When riding normally, your pony's hindlegs should follow the tracks of its forelegs. Some good exercises for making your pony supple are ones where it moves its hindlegs off the track of its forelegs. This is called lateral work. The pony has to bend its body and use its hindlegs strongly.

Turn on the forehand

Teach your pony to turn on the forehand as shown below. Hold its head still. Tap its side so its hindlegs move away from you. The forelegs will go up and down on the spot.

Now give the pony the same aids from the saddle. Your hands stop it from moving forwards. Your right leg behind the girth pushes his hindquarters around.

22

Shoulder-in

A shoulder-in is an advanced lateral exercise for experienced riders and well-trained ponies. Your teacher will tell you when you are ready to learn it.

The pony's spine is bent as if to walk in a circle, but the pony moves forwards on a straight line. The head and neck are turned away from the direction it is going. This helps the rider to gain control of the hindquarters.

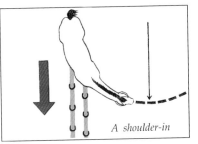

A shoulder-in

Half-halt

A half-halt is another advanced technique that helps a rider to get a pony balanced and attentive before asking the pony to turn or change pace. The rider sits deep in the saddle and closes his or her legs on the girth. The hands on the reins stop the pony from going faster. The hindquarters come under the pony and weight is taken off the forelegs, making the pony balanced and ready.

A half-halt is an almost invisible way to get a pony's attention.

23

Jumping

Jumping is exciting, but you should not start until you feel
secure and can control your pony at a walk, a trot and a canter.

Trotting poles

Trotting poles develop balance
and confidence before you try a
jump. Start by walking over one
pole. Add more, one at a time.
The distance between them
depends on your pony's stride –
your teacher will help you.

Then try going over the poles
at a steady rising trot. When
you feel safe doing this, place a
set of low cross poles (see
opposite) about 2.5m (8ft)
from the last pole. Trot down
the line and over the jump.

*Lean forwards
a little.*

*Trot over the middle
of the poles, keeping
a steady rhythm.*

The right way to jump

Sit calmly upright
in the saddle as
your pony
approaches the
jump. Encourage
the pony with
your legs and let
its stride settle
into a rhythm.

Approach

1. Let your pony
lower its head, to
judge the jump. Lean
forwards as the
pony pushes off.

Take-off

2. Keep close to the
saddle, and do not
stand up in the
stirrups. Give your
pony plenty of rein.

24

Making your own jumps

Here are some ways to make simple jumps. Only use safe materials which will not hurt a pony's legs if it hits them. Change the jumps and move them around often so that a pony does not get bored.

Tree trunk
Trim off any stumps of branches and saw off any sharp edges which might catch a pony's feet.

Straw bales
Set up a single row of straw bales, end to end, or a double row with a third row on top. Put some at the sides.

Car tyres
Ask at a garage for six or eight old car tyres. Hang them on a pole. Put another pole on the ground in front of the jump.

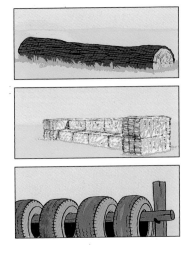

Oil drums
Ask at a garage for large, empty oil drums. Here are three ways you can use them.

These are called cross poles.

In the air	Landing	Away

3. Keep your knees on the saddle. Do not let your legs slip back or you will unbalance the pony.

4. The front feet hit the ground hard. Take some of the strain by moving back a little.

5. Take control as soon as you land. The whole jump should be smooth and flowing.

Better jumping

Most ponies enjoy jumping. For jumping, a pony should be at least five years old and in good condition. The height a pony can jump depends on his physique, temperament and experience.

Always reward your pony with a pat.

Jumping is strenuous and you must both be fit.

Have your stirrups a hole or two shorter for jumping.

Ask your teacher to help you measure the length of your pony's stride.

You need to make sure the pony will reach the take-off point in a balanced stride. Count the strides as you ride up to a jump. A marker and a pole, arranged as on the right, will help you.

Two strides   *One stride*

The wrong way to jump

The rider has been left behind. His weight is in the wrong place.

The rider has moved too far forwards, too soon. He will unbalance the pony.

Types of jump

Different jumps
test the skills
of pony and
rider.

Upright jump
The pony should approach an upright jump with its head low, to judge height and take-off.

Spread jump
Approach a little faster than for upright jumps, to help clear the width as well as the height.

Parallel jump
This is a difficult fence which needs a big jump, from an accurate take-off point.

Water jump
Approach at a strong canter. The pony must jump high to clear the length.

The rider's legs have slipped back and up. He cannot control the pony.

The rider is looking down. You should always look up and beyond, to the next jump.

Grooming and feeding

Ponies need to be brushed to keep their coats healthy. If the pony is kept in a stable, groom it every day as described opposite. If it is living outdoors, then just follow Step 1. This will keep the coat clean without removing its natural waterproof protection.

A dandy brush has stiff bristles to clean off mud and sweat.

Body brush for removing dust and dirt from the coat.

Hoof pick for cleaning out the feet.

Use a plastic curry comb to clean the body brush.

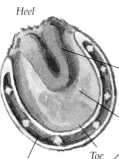

Heel

This soft part is called the frog.

Most of the inside is hard horn.

Toe

Metal shoe to stop hoof from getting worn down.

Cleaning out the hooves

Hooves should be picked out before and after each ride. Run your hand down the pony's leg and say, "Up". Support the hoof firmly. Use the hoof pick from heel to toe, beside the frog. Be careful not to dig the hook into the frog.

Feeding

Ponies have small stomachs for their size so they need to eat little and often. Hay replaces grass for stabled ponies but they may need other types of food in addition to hay.

Pony cubes are a dried, ready-made mixture of foods.

Barley is an energy food.

Hay is dried grass. It should smell sweet and feel crisp.

Sugar beet pulp needs to be soaked for 24 hours before feeding.

Oats give energy. Too many oats can make ponies hot and excitable.

Brushing the coat

1. Brush off mud and dried sweat with a dandy brush. It is hard, so avoid sensitive areas. Use short, firm strokes.

2. Use the body brush in long strokes all over. After every few strokes, clean the brush with the curry comb.

3. Wipe around the eyes and nostrils with a damp sponge. Clean under the tail with a sponge kept just for this job.

4. Brush the mane and tail with the body brush. Brush a few hairs at a time, being careful not to break any hairs.

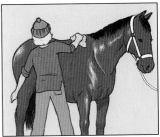

5. Put a coat of hoof oil on the hoof wall. You can oil the sole and frog if they are clean, to help stop them from cracking.

6. Finally, you can rub the pony all over with a clean cloth so the coat is smooth and shiny.

Stabling and living out

If you ride a lot and your pony needs to be really fit, it is best to keep it stabled. There is no need to keep the pony inside all the time. A few hours a day in a field will keep it happy and easier to manage.

The stable

Your stable should be a loose box or strong shed with a divided door, at least 3m x 4m (10ft x 13ft). Rough concrete makes a good stable floor, as it will stop the pony slipping. The floor should slope very slightly down to a drain. In winter, your pony might need a rug for warmth.

Ponies looking over a divided stable door.

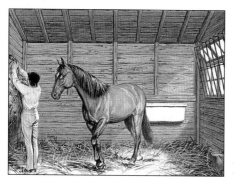

Bedding

Cover the floor with deep bedding. Straw, wood shavings and shredded paper are all good forms of bedding. Remove droppings and wet bedding every day. Add clean bedding when needed.

Putting on a rug

1. Throw the folded rug over the pony's withers. Then unfold it over its back.

2. Pull the rug into place, so that it hangs evenly. Fasten the front buckle.

3. Fasten the straps around the middle, enough to keep the rug in place.

Keeping a pony at grass

A pony kept in a field needs food, water and shelter.
The field should be fenced with post-and-rail fencing,
strong hedges, or plain wire (not barbed wire).

Pick droppings up regularly. Ponies like to eat
short, juicy grass, not the long, coarse grass that
grows where droppings have fallen. Also, ponies
get worms from the eggs that live in droppings.

Check your pony for injuries and pick out its feet at least once a day.

A post-and-rail fence is strong and ponies cannot injure themselves on it.

An open, south facing shed provides shelter.

Poisonous plants

Search your field for poisonous plants,
such as those shown here. Uproot and
burn them. Fence off any harmful
shrubs or trees.

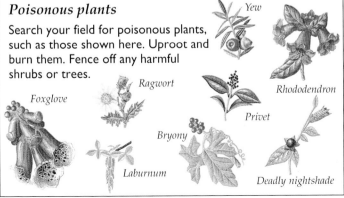

Yew

Rhododendron

Foxglove

Ragwort

Privet

Bryony

Laburnum

Deadly nightshade

Index

This book is based on material previously published in *The Usborne Guide to Riding and Pony Care, Starting Riding* and the *Usborne Spotter's Guide: Horses and Ponies.*

First published in 1995 by Usborne Publishing Ltd, Usborne House, 83-85 Saffron Hill, London EC1N 8RT, England.